The

Adventures

Of

Elbert

And

Leopoldina

Other books by Dorothy Kubik:

A Free Soil – A Free People:
The Anti-Rent War in Delaware County, New York

and

West Through the Catskills:
The Story of the Susquehanna Turnpike

MAY BE ORDERED FROM:

Echo Farm Publications   607-865-8351
8058 County Highway 26, Hamden, New York 13782

OR:

Purple Mountain Press   1 - 800- 325-2665
PO Box 309, Fleischmanns, NY 12430-0309

The

Adventures

of

Elbert

and

Leopoldina

To: Dr. Elizabeth Dennis –
With many thanks for your care
and sensitivity. Best wishes for joy,
peace, and success.

Dorothy Kubik *Dorothy Kubik*
April 18, 2008

Illustrations by Annie James

Echo Farm Publications, Hamden, New York

The Adventures of Elbert and Leopoldina
First Soft Cover Edition - 2006

Echo Farm Publications
8058 County Highway 26
Hamden, New York 13782
607-865-8351

Library of Congress Control Number: TXu-278-451

ISBN#: 978-0-9790775-1-7

Cover design by Annie James

Produced in the United States of America on acid-free
paper.

Touchstone Consulting, Touchstone Graphics, and Touchstone Press
(all divisions of **Touchstone Communications**)
had roles in planning, typesetting & layout, and print production of this book.
see: Touchstonegraphics.com
353 Main Street, Suite 1D, Oneonta, NY 13820   •   (607) 437-0000

For:

Mary Ann

Marie and Ron

And

In Memory of

Ken

Table of Contents

Chapter 1

Magic in the Air

Something strange was singing in the wind that June morning. Leopoldina, Skip Tapper's pet goose, could feel it rustling her feathers as she wandered over the front lawn, relishing the tasty green grass after a long winter diet of cracked corn and oats. Between nibbles, she raised her long neck and turned this way and that in short sharp jerks.

There it was again, tickling her ears, sliding down her throat, stirring up her blood, making her heart thump faster. It wasn't just the music of long warm days in the summer sun. It was an unfamiliar combination of notes, some high and teasing, some low and mysterious. Together they created a stirring melody that urged her to come swiftly, for something exciting lay beyond the front lawn and down the road.

Just as Leopoldina was about to go flying across the lawn toward the road, the screen door banged. She turned to see her faithful friend, Elbert the beagle, come racing across the lawn, wagging his tail vigorously. Elbert had been nosing around the edge of the meadow that stretched beyond the lawn. But the sight and sound of Skip, coming out the back door with that bright yellow bowl, was enough to make him forget everything else.

"Come and get it, Elbert," Skip called as he set the bowl down beside the back steps. In a second, Elbert buried his nose in the bowl.

"You're next, Leopoldina," Skip added, as he started back into the house.

Skip was a tall thin boy with thick curly carrot-red hair, a generous sprinkling of freckles, and sea-green eyes. His jeans, whether old or new, always seemed to have a tear or a smudge of mud. For Skip was an explorer, and all the woods and fields were home to him With his untied sneaker laces bouncing around his feet and his green and white baseball cap slung backwards on his head, he set out to find adventure under every rock and to make new friends with every creature with whom he shared his world.

Leopoldina and Elbert lived with the Tappers on a small farm on Finch Hollow Road in the foothills of the Catskill Mountains. Skip's parents had bought the farm five years earlier from an old farmer and his wife. It was set in a narrow valley between two mountains. Meadows for grazing and fields of corn and alfalfa rolled in gentle waves from the edge of the lawn to the foot of the mountains, broken only by an old apple orchard.

Beyond the fields, a woodlot sat against the base of the mountain. On the other side of the valley, about a mile down the road, New York City's Cannonsville Reservoir lay between the mountains, catching on its glimmering surface pictures of the high steep hills that ringed it.

The family lived in the big old farmhouse with its 14 rooms, wide front porch, and multi-paned windows. A short distance from the house stood the old red barn. Its roof was sagging, and the stanchions were empty, waiting for cows that would never return. Above, the hay mow lay, sprinkled with stray wisps and clumps of hay left over from a mowing long ago. Next to the barn was the milk house where pans of milk had once filled the shelves along the walls. Now Skip's dad used the space for his carpentry tools and woodworking projects. Nearby, the horse barn, now a garage, housed the Tappers' car and truck.

Skip came out the back door again with another dish in his hand. "Come on, Leopoldina," he called, bending down slightly and extending the dish.

Leopoldina primly cocked her head and looked up into the dish as if to say, "I'll have to consider this." After all, the taste of fresh green grass was still sweet in her mouth. But she continued to follow the moving dish into the enclosure she knew as home. Mr. Tapper had built her a comfortable coop fenced in with wire to discourage any adventuresome streak that might come over her when the family was away. But to her credit, it must be said that Leopoldina had never ventured beyond the lawn, even when Skip let her roam freely.

Now, however, a wind was singing in her ears and pushing at her tail. There was no telling where it would lead her, though at the moment, her sights were set only on the dish that Skip set down on the grass inside her pen. While she was occupied with her breakfast, Skip closed the gate and loosely slipped the wire loop over the fence post.

Leopoldina nibbled daintily at the cracked corn and oat mash for a few seconds. Then she turned her attention to the grass again. She was interrupted in her grazing by voices running across the lawn and a car door banging.

"Hurry, Skip, or we'll be late," Mrs. Tapper called from the car window.

"It'll take just a minute," Skip called back as he ran into the house and emerged a few seconds later, bat and mitt in hand, his cap slung backwards on his head, his shoelaces flying around his running feet.

Elbert ran alongside him, sure he would be invited for a ride. But when Skip reached the car, he climbed into the front seat and banged the door behind him. "You be good, Elbert, and help Dad," Skip called out the window as the car rolled slowly down the driveway, the tires crunching on the gravel.

With sinking spirits, Elbert watched the car go down the driveway, stop, then turn down the road to the reservoir. With his tail drooping and his face cast down, Elbert dragged himself across the lawn to the front porch. He snuggled into his favorite spot between the rhododendron bushes by the steps and began to cry into his paws.

Often when Skip went away in the car, he invited Elbert into the back seat where Elbert would sit close to Skip and watch the countryside zip by. But today, Skip had not even patted him on the head or promised his dog that he would soon return. Leopoldina had little sympathy for Elbert. She was used to being left at home. Besides, that was no way to act, especially on a delicious summer day when a teasing wind was ruffling your feathers and tickling your down, a wind that was singing, "Come, fly with me!"

Leopoldina began to bombard Elbert with a loud steady honking. At first, Elbert merely opened his eyes for a moment, then went back to his whimpering. But Leopoldina persisted. Finally, Elbert raised his head and looked around quizzically. Not observing anything unusual in the immediate vicinity, he decided, though he was in no mood for play, that he had better see what she wanted.

He dragged himself across the lawn toward her pen. As he approached, Leopoldina went to the gate and honked again. Elbert knew then that she wanted to get out, so he obligingly pushed his nose against the edge of the gate where he found a small crack. The gate moved a bit but not enough to get his head in. After several unsuccessful attempts, he stood on his hind legs and tried the top of the gate. He pushed until the wire loop, slung loosely over the post, gave way and the gate flew open.

Leopoldina honked gratefully and marched out. Spurred on by the magical music of the wind, she sailed swiftly to the driveway. There she stopped and turned back to Elbert, who had stood watching her. The look in her eye meant she expected him to follow her.

Suddenly, Elbert felt it, too—that breeze playing around his nose like butterflies teasing him to catch them. It smelled like wild flowers and sparkling water and freshly mown hay, and it tasted like a thick juicy bone.

With a leap, he bounded down the driveway as if he were pursuing those elusive butterflies. When he reached the road, he stopped and waited for Leopoldina. Together they set off down the road. But the scent was too much for Elbert. Again he bolted away, racing toward the bottom of the hill. Leopoldina followed, half waddling, half flying until she caught up with him where he waited for her at the STOP sign at the bottom of the hill.

They stood together and peered up and down the road, which ran like a ragged gray crayon line between the trees and bushes along the reservoir: Leopoldina in her fine white dress, Elbert in his motley suit of brown, black, and white.

The road lay still, gleaming roughly in the morning sun. But every now and then, a car or truck came along, swift and sharp and sure, stirring up little eddies of dust that settled again into the silence. Straight ahead the reservoir glimmered in the morning sun like a gigantic blue gem set in the green of the surrounding mountains.

Leopoldina and Elbert looked first to the right, then to the left. Then they hurried across the road and into the bushes on the bank of the reservoir. Elbert led the way. Leopoldina had quite a struggle to get through the undergrowth, but she followed close in Elbert's wake. Finally, they broke through at the edge of the reservoir. Without looking around, they both lunged for the water, lapping it up intently.

Their thirst quenched, they looked up and surveyed the scene. The wide glimmering surface of the reservoir had disappeared. They were standing on the bank of a narrow, swiftly flowing river, hemmed in by thickly grown banks of elderberry bushes and wild grasses.

Where were they? What had happened to their world? Elbert sniffed the air. What was that strange scent that was floating on the breeze? It smelled like strawberries ripening in the sun, or was it the wet earth after a summer shower? In it was something he knew and something he did not know.

Leopoldina rearranged her wings and looked about uncertainly. Then she heard the singing in the wind again, only this time it seemed a little slow and sad, like petals falling from a faded rose.

Confused, the two travelers looked around, trying to find the bank down which they had come. But that had disappeared, too. Elbert knew that they had to keep moving if they were going to find the way home. So he started off along the river bank with Leopoldina following clumsily behind him. They did not know that they were going farther and farther from home with each step, deep into the world of a hundred years ago.

Chapter 2

Nathaniel

They had walked a short distance when Elbert suddenly stopped and sniffed the air. A people scent with an unfamiliar cool shading came from downstream. It was not like any people scents he had ever known. But the travelers went on until they reached a bend in the river.

There they came upon a thin, long-legged boy sitting on a large rock that jutted out over the water. He was wearing faded patched overalls, a collarless white shirt open at the neck, and a large straw hat with a ragged brim. A fishing pole dangled from his hands, and he was watching the water intently.

Elbert barked to announce their presence. The boy turned. He pushed back the hat, which had shaded his tanned face, and studied them. "Where did you come from?" he asked at last.

Elbert barked again, as if to say, "And who are you?" Leopoldina followed with a short uncertain honk. Elbert took half a step back. He was unsure what to make of this human. He seemed very much like Skip but the scent was wrong.

The boy looked at Leopoldina and laughed. "What a fat goose! I bet you 'scaped from the Widow Blair because she was getting you ready for the roasting pan."

His words sent a shiver of fright through Leopoldina. She wanted to run up to him and hassle him to death, but the strangeness of the whole scene confused her. All she could do was honk loudly and steadily in his direction. Elbert, however, encouraged by the tone of the boy's voice and a tantalizing smell, made his way through the undergrowth and up the rock where the boy sat.

Next to the boy lay six fish lined up one behind the other on a string. As Elbert nosed them, the boy turned sharply and grabbed the string of fish.

"Hey, this is our dinner," he said. "You stay away from it, Rover."

Elbert backed away while the boy turned his attention to a tug on his line. He pulled it in and took off the end a struggling trout. "Look at that! Isn't she a beauty?" he said. He looked at Elbert, who was wagging his tail hopefully. "Not for you, Rover. But if you come home with me, I can find you a nice juicy bone." Elbert wagged his tail more vigorously. Then he watched the boy add the newly caught fish to the six on his string.

With his fishing pole in one hand and the string of fish in the other, the boy set off along the river through the tall grasses and bushes hugging its banks. Elbert and Leopoldina followed. The boy did not seem threatening, and they might get some food.

Finally, they reached a bridge over the river. They crossed the bridge and continued on down a dirt road which was wet and filled with puddles. As they walked, they left three sets of prints—four dog prints, two goose prints, and the boy's bare feet.

Leopoldina began to feel hungry and stopped every now and then to nibble at grass along the road. Elbert felt the pangs of hunger, too, but he smelled nothing suitable to eat except the fish the boy was carrying. He began to lag behind and was about to give up following the boy when they turned in at another narrower dirt road that led across the fields to a house and a barn set against a hill.

Suddenly, two large dogs came rushing down the road toward them, one a white dog with brown spots and a shaggy coat. The other was a sleek-looking black. They greeted the boy wildly, jumping all over him. He transferred his catch of fish to his other hand and petted them. "You were lonesome, weren't you?" he said as he rubbed their necks.

The dogs then turned their attention to Elbert and Leopoldina, barking fiercely at the two strangers. Leopoldina and Elbert had already begun to back away, but the boy called to the dogs in a firm voice, "No, Rusty! No, Shep! Come with me."

The dogs quieted down and turned to follow the boy, but not before they had cast several more doubtful glances at these strange newcomers.

The group proceeded along the road that cut through fields thick with clover and hay. They drew closer to the house, which looked like Skip's, but it had a worn and tired look, and needed a fresh coat of paint. On the north side, a line of tall firs protected it from the fierce winds of winter. To its left, stood a large barn and several other smaller buildings, all painted red.

When they reached the house, a short sturdy woman came out the back door, wiping her hands on a white apron which she wore over a long dark calico dress. Her brown hair was piled on top of her head and held with large combs, though strands of it had escaped and were sticking to her wet forehead and cheeks.

"Nathaniel, I'm so glad you're back. I was worried about you. What kept you so long?" she asked, wiping her face with the

15

edge of the apron and tucking in the loose strands of hair.

"Look at what a catch I had, Mother," he answered, handing her the fish.

"That's fine, Nat. Just in time for dinner. But what kept you so long?"

"Oh, the fish weren't bitin' too good at first," he said.

Just then his mother looked up and saw Elbert and Leopoldina waiting a distance away, not sure of their welcome. "Why, Nat, where did you get that goose and dog?" she asked.

"They came up to the fishing hole and just followed me home."

"We must find out who owns them."

"I promised Rover a nice juicy bone. Do you think he can have one?"

"Most certainly. Poor fellow looks starved and thirsty. Give the goose something, too," she added, turning to go back into the house. "Your father is going into the village this afternoon. He can inquire around if anyone is missing a goose and a beagle."

Nathaniel followed his mother to the back door. "I didn't know Father was going to the village today," he said.

"Well, he just decided that he had better see the blacksmith about getting Nellie shod, and he'll look into getting another horse to replace Libby."

"Is Reuben getting the colt, too?" Nathaniel asked.

"He hasn't gathered enough money yet for that," his mother answered as they disappeared into the house.

Chapter 3

New Friends

Leopoldina and Elbert did not have to wait long before Nathaniel brought out a bowl of water, which they promptly lapped up. Then Elbert set to work on a dish of tasty meat and a large juicy bone. Leopoldina munched on a dish of corn and potato peelings. Then she sought out the thick green grass near the pond, which mirrored a bright blue summer sky.

Around the lawn between the house and barn, a flock of chickens wandered, pecking here and there and cackling as they went. When they spotted Leopoldina, they started to come toward her. Fear gripped her, but she mounted the best defense she knew. She ran at them with a steady honking, aiming for the biggest and most aggressive hen. Then Leopoldina began to nip at the hen and chase her. The hen flew off wildly with great squawking, and the whole band took off in a flurry of dust and feathers.

Their dinners finished, the two dogs came over to investigate Elbert. At first, they tried to take his bone from him, but he defended it tenaciously. Soon the dogs were all romping over the lawn while Leopoldina sought out the quiet of the pond.

At last, Nathaniel and his father came across the yard to the barn. His father then led a powerful looking brown horse from the barn toward a wagon that stood nearby. Nathaniel's father was a tall, strong man with firm muscles and a face brown from work in the sun. His weathered hands worked deftly as he hitched the horse to the wagon.

"Go get them, Nat," he said, gesturing toward Elbert, who had hastened to join them.

Nat let down the back of the wagon. "Come on, Rover," he said. "We're going to see if we can find out who lost you and your friend."

Obediently, Elbert jumped onto the bed of the wagon, his tail wagging happily in expectation of some great adventure.

At that moment, a girl, slightly younger than Nathaniel, came running from the house, her thick brown braids bouncing up and down. "Where are they?" she cried. "I want to see them before you take them away."

Meanwhile, Leopoldina had hurried up from the pond. When she looked around for Elbert and did not see him, she began to run toward the house, honking excitedly.

"There you are, you silly goose," the girl laughed. "Aren't you the cutest ever!"

Nathaniel scooped up the honking Leopoldina and carried her to the wagon.

"Where are you taking her?" the girl asked, climbing into the wagon.

"To the village to see if anyone will claim her," Nathaniel answered, getting into the wagon and placing Leopoldina into a crate with wooden slats. Leopoldina's heart was beating rapidly. As Nathaniel put her into the crate she saw Elbert standing there, looking at her mournfully. He wagged his tail slowly and steadily, as if to let her know he was still her devoted friend.

"Why can't we keep her?" the girl asked.

"Because she's not ours. Now get out, Betsy, so we can go." Nathaniel answered.

Betsy jumped to the ground and then glanced up to see Nathaniel fastening Leopoldina's crate. "Don't lock her in, Nat," she said. "How would you like it if someone locked you in a box?"

"You're a pest, Betsy," Nathaniel said as he climbed into the front seat beside his father.

"Go help your mother finish the dishes, Betsy," her father said.

"Oh, Papa! Can't we keep the goose? If someone else gets her, she'll be killed and roasted."

"How do you know the same fate wouldn't befall her here?" her father asked with a smile.

Betsy ran to him. "Please, Papa," she pleaded, looking up at him, sitting high up on the wagon, reins in hand, ready to start.

Her father softened. "Well, if no one claims her, she will be yours. But first we must see if she belongs to anyone else. We can't keep her if she isn't ours."

"I hope no one claims her," Betsy answered. "Then she'll be my very own pet and I'll call her Silly Goose."

Nathaniel's father pulled on the reins, and the horse set off at a brisk trot down the road in little swirls of dust, for the noon sun had already dried the puddles from last night's rain.

They crossed the bridge over the river and turned down another dusty road, riding under shady trees. They passed meadows where cows lay scattered about, and fields of timothy and alfalfa, inching their way toward the reaper's scythe, and acres of corn and oats, their young stalks growing taller and stronger in the summer sun. On the left, just beyond the road, the river murmured busily along its way. Finally, they reached the village of Cannonsville.

Chapter 4

A Trip to Town

They rode into Main Street in the shade of maples and hemlocks that crowded close to the road. On the right side of the road sat spacious houses, mostly white, with wrap-around front porches. On the left, the river flowed busily and cheerfully around Council Island where, according to legend, the Indians used to gather for their council meetings.

A slight jog in Main Street brought them into the business district, where several merchants had signs reading "Boots, Shoes, Dry Goods, and General Merchandise." Sandwiched between them on the corner of Cemetery Street and Main

Street, stood the Methodist Episcopal Church with its steeple watching over the village like a stern guardian. Pulling up in front of Gillet's Store, Nathaniel's father said, "I must stop here for your mother's shoes, Nat. You wait here. I won't be a minute."

Elbert climbed up onto the wagon seat and together he and Nathaniel studied the quiet afternoon street. A wagon and horse were tied in front of Owens' Store. Two women came out of the store, carrying baskets filled with their purchases. Their long dresses swayed lightly just above the bluestone sidewalk that gave pedestrians some relief from the dust and mud of the road.

Just as Nathaniel's father emerged from Gillet's, a short stocky middle-aged man in a black suit and crumpled white shirt crossed the street and came toward him.

"Hello, there, Alex," he called.

"Why, Dr. Cottrell," Nathaniel's father answered extending his hand for a hearty handshake. "Good to see you."

"What are you doing in town this fine sunny afternoon? I'd expect you to be haying it."

"Business, Dr. Cottrell, business that wouldn't wait for rain or shine. But Reuben and the boys are taking care of the haying. I expect they'll take in quite a load before I get home."

"Reuben's grown up to be quite a man," Dr. Cottrell said.

"That he has. I can put him in charge any time, and I know the work will get done."

While Dr. Cottrell and Nathaniel's father were talking, Elbert climbed back into the wagon bed and nosed around the crate where Leopoldina was imprisoned, but he could find no way to free her. Sadly, he lay down close to her, his face on his paws, and stared mournfully at the bottom of the wagon.

Nathaniel's father climbed back into the wagon and started off again down the rutted street. In a short time, he stopped at a small white building with many tall windows and the letters B-A-N-K printed in gold above the double front doors.

"I may be a while, Nat," he said, jumping down from the wagon. "Watch the animals carefully."

Nathaniel climbed into the wagon bed. "How are you doing back here, Rover?" he asked, rubbing Elbert's neck and back. Elbert wagged his tail and licked Nathaniel's face.

The sound of metal hitting against metal drew Nathaniel's attention to the collar around Elbert's neck. Examining it, he found three silver-colored metal tags. "Say, what's this?" he muttered. Two of the tags had numbers and letters that he could not make sense of, but the third was clear— too clear. It read: "Elbert, Finch Hollow Road, Walton, NY, 607-865-5402."

Nathaniel drew in his breath and held it for a moment. "Do you belong to someone on Finch Hollow Road, Rover?" he asked, looking into Elbert's eyes.

Elbert answered with a questioning look and wagged his tail slowly, hesitantly, waiting for some warm words.

Nathaniel examined the tag again. "We have got to get rid of this, Rover, 'cause you are going to be my dog, and we are going to be great friends."

Overcome with joy, Elbert pounced upon Nathaniel, knocking him over and licking his face.

"Hey, wait a minute, Rover," Nathaniel laughed as he rolled on the wagon floor with Elbert.

Finally, he sat up and Elbert watched him, ready for more play. "We'll have great times going hunting. Would you like to go hunting for rabbits?"

Elbert wagged his tail vigorously and looked up at Nathaniel as if to say, "I'm ready. Let's go."

Leopoldina wanted to be part of the excitement, too. She began to honk and move restlessly against the restraining slats of the crate.

Nathaniel turned toward her. "Oh, so you would like to go, too? Well, you wouldn't be much help hunting. You will end up in the roasting pan, likely as not," he said.

At the sound of these comfortless words, Leopoldina's heart beat faster. She rumpled up her feathers and honked again. That recalled Elbert to his friend's sad plight. He nosed around the edges of the crate and pushed against the lid, but it was too securely fastened to budge even an inch.

"Your friend will have to stay in there until we get to the Widow Blair's," Nathaniel said to Elbert.

Just then, Nathaniel's father emerged from the bank, climbed into the wagon, and set off down the street. Their next stop was the blacksmith's.

Jehiel Benjamin, the blacksmith, kept his shop on the corner of Maple and Main Streets. Nearby stood Mr. Leal's flour and feed mill, and back of the mill, along Trout Creek, Mr. J.A. Kenyon operated his tannery, where hides were turned into leather "of the finest quality," as Mr. Kenyon said.

They drove into the rutted yard in front of the blacksmith shop. Scattered about were wagons, buggies, and various pieces of farm equipment. The small gray shop seemed lost, standing in the middle of the jumble that had grown up around it.

Inside, Mr. Benjamin, in his leather apron, stood at the fire in his forge, a shower of red sparks dancing in the air in front of him. He was a tall strong man with thick black hair and beard, and a round ruddy face. His presence made the small shop seem even smaller than it was. He glanced up as Nathaniel and his father came through the doorway.

"Why, hello there, Mr. Nichol," he said. A red-hot horseshoe glowed in the dim light. Then it sizzled as he plunged it into a tub of cold water. "How's the haying going?"

"Right fine," Nathaniel's father answered. "Reuben and the boys are working at it now."

"Reuben's getting to be quite a man. Has he got his colt yet from Mr. Fyffe?"

"No, I expect he's steadily adding to his savings and should soon be able to purchase it."

"Then he'll bring me more work, too," Mr. Benjamin added with a laugh. "Need Nellie shod today?"

"Yes, if you can do her now. Say, isn't that Mr. Fyffe's wagon there on the side of the shop?"

"Sure 'tis. It's Buster's shoes I'm working on right now."

"Where's Mr. Fyffe? I hoped to see him today."

"Went across the street to the hardware store," Mr. Benjamin said.

"Tell him when he returns that I want to see him. Nat and I are walking down to the Widow Blair's while you get Nellie shod. By the way, do you know of anyone who lost a beagle and a goose?"

31

"No, I can't say as I do," he answered slowly as he walked toward the door with Nathaniel and his father. He looked toward the wagon where Elbert was nervously moving from one end to the other. "Where did you find them?"

"They followed Nat home this forenoon," Nathaniel's father replied.

"Let me have a look at them," Mr. Benjamin said, walking toward the wagon.

Elbert began to bark as Mr. Benjamin approached, and Leopoldina added several loud honks.

Mr. Benjamin studied the animals for a moment and then said with a grin. "Like as not, the Widow Blair will take the goose if you can't find its home. But I'd like that dog if you don't find his owner."

Nathaniel eyed his father apprehensively, and Elbert echoed his fear with another bark. "You said I could keep him if we didn't find where he belongs," Nathaniel said.

"I did?" his father said. "I know I half promised the goose to Betsy." Then he turned to Mr. Benjamin. "I think Nat and the dog have already become fast friends, Jehiel. You'll have to find yourself another dog."

"Finders keepers, I guess," Mr. Benjamin commented with a laugh as he unhitched Nellie.

"Come on, Rover," Nathaniel whispered, climbing into the wagon for Elbert. His father picked up the crate with Leopoldina, who began to honk excitedly, and they set off down the road, crossing Trout Creek where it flowed into the river. They passed several houses similar to the ones they had gone by at the other end of the village. Then they reached the edge of the village where the Widow Blair lived.

The little brown shingled house looked as frazzled as its owner with a loose shutter here, a cracked window pane there, and a broken rocker on the paint-worn front porch. A brown picket fence with gaping holes fenced in the yard where the Widow's flock of geese often sauntered with a proprietary air.

As Nathaniel and his father walked through the gate, they saw the Widow in the backyard, taking in the wash, so they cut across the grass toward her.

The Widow Blair was a short plump woman with a rosy complexion and a great double chin. She had an exasperated expression on her face, as if she had just been chasing a goose and hadn't been able to catch it. Her wiry gray hair protruded along the edge of her ruffled white cap.

She had just bent down to lay a dry towel in her clothes basket when she caught sight of them coming across the lawn. She dropped the towel and hastened toward them. "Oh, Mr. Nichol! How glad I am to see you!" she exclaimed, clasping her hands together.

"How have you been, Mrs. Blair?" Nathaniel's father asked.

She shook her head mournfully. "Oh, it is so hard for a poor widow to get by, but I do the best I can." She glanced down at the crate. "What have you got there?" she asked.

Before Nathaniel's father could answer, Leopoldina responded with a frightened honk.

"A goose? For me?" she asked.

"It followed Nat home today, and we thought perhaps it was yours," he said.

"Oh, dearie me, I hope not," she said, throwing up her hands and rushing toward the back gate, which led out into the meadow where her flock was wandering.

She ran out the gate and began to round up the geese, calling loudly and shooing them inside the yard. As they filed in, the geese set up a great outcry, unhappy at this interruption of their afternoon meanderings.

Elbert, meanwhile, had been nosing around the side of the house. But the noise brought him back to the scene. At first, he stood for a moment, startled by the flock of Leopoldinas coming toward him. Then, half ready for battle, half prepared to run, if necessary, he began to bark at these strange counterfeits. A large gander suddenly headed straight for him, honking and nipping at Elbert as he turned and ran for the front yard.

"Rover! Rover! Come back here!" Nat cried, taking off after his friend, while Leopoldina set up another frightened outcry.

As the geese came running into the yard, the Widow, breathless, began to count, "One, two, three, four . . . eight, nine, ten. They're all here, Mr. Nichol," she said. She peered into Leopoldina's crate. "That's a fine looking goose—nice and fat. My sister and her daughter are coming from Chicago to visit me soon, and that goose would make a tasty morsel to serve. And I need feathers to finish the pillows that Amanda Jennings' mother wants to give her for a wedding present."

Leopoldina heard death in the Widow's words and began to honk fiercely.

"What are you asking for her?" the Widow asked.

"Oh, I'm not selling her," Nathaniel's father replied. "I promised her to Betsy if no one claimed her."

The Widow shook her head. "She would indeed make a tasty morsel. If you change your mind, I will buy her from you."

"I will still ask Mr. Fyffe and Mr. Sprague if they know of anyone who might have lost her. And, perhaps, if Betsy does keep her, she will tire of taking care of a goose, and then you can have her."

Leopoldina honked again as she strained harder against the crate. Elbert, who was clinging close to Nathaniel, looked up at her with puzzled eyes. He knew that she felt threatened, but he could not see what the threat was. The other geese had lost interest in the strangers and had begun to wander back through the open gate into the meadow.

"Is there anything you need done?" Nathaniel's father asked as they turned to leave.

"Oh, yes, Mr. Nichol, my roof. It's leaking badly. Come, I'll show you."

She led them through the kitchen into a dining room darkened with drawn drapes, up an open stairway, and into a bedroom at the head of the stairs. A large four-poster bed covered with a blue and white woven coverlet was pushed close against the window. Between it and a small wooden chest of drawers stood a bucket partially filled with water.

The Widow pointed to a wet spot on the ceiling above the bucket. "See how it is staining the wallpaper. And the plaster will come falling down if it isn't fixed soon."

Nathaniel's father studied the spot. Then he turned to the Widow. "I'll send Reuben to fix it as soon as we have a break in the haying."

The Widow folded her hands and pleaded. "Oh, please, Mr. Nichol, let him come before the next rain."

"Perhaps we can spare him for an afternoon soon. Nat here is getting to be a big boy, too, and he's quite a help around the farm."

"Oh, thank you, thank you, Mr. Nichol," she exclaimed over and over as she escorted them down the stairs to the front door.

Chapter 5

Mystery Tags

During the next several weeks, Elbert and Leopoldina led a delightful carefree existence as Rover and Silly Goose.

From the first stirrings of morning when the rooster crowed until the farm quieted down at evening, Elbert followed at Nathaniel's heels. He swept the barn with his friend, chasing the broom from side to side. Together they carried milk to the buttery, where Nathaniel's mother poured it into low wide pans set on shelves about the walls. Then they watered the horses and fed the chickens.

In the bright summer sunshine, Elbert romped in the freshly cut hay before Nathaniel and the men threw it into the hay wagon with huge pitchforks, the long sharp prongs gleaming fiercely in the sun. Only when the men unloaded the hay into the hay mow which was high in the barn, did Elbert have to stay outdoors and watch from a distance.

But, on some days, when the daily chores were done, he and Nathaniel would set off on an excursion. Perhaps they would sit by the river while Nathaniel caught fish for the family's dinner. Sometimes they roamed the fields and woods, where Elbert ran his beagle heart out after rabbits or woodchucks. Sometimes they would play games with Elbert running swiftly for the ball that Nathaniel threw. And sometimes they just hiked and hiked and studied the creatures of the woods.

Leopoldina's days were less exciting, but she was delighted with every moment of attention from Betsy. She submitted to being dressed with bonnets and aprons and bows. She was particularly proud of the bright blue satin ribbon that Betsy tied around her neck. She would walk about the yard, bobbing her head back and forth to draw everyone's attention to her finery. And with the thick rich grass around the pond and the pans of grain and potato peelings that Betsy fed her, she grew fatter and fatter.

When visitors came to the farm, they were greeted by everyone (except Nathaniel and Betsy) with the question: "Do you know anyone who lost a goose and a dog?"

Nathaniel and Betsy would bite their lips and hold their breaths until the visitors would shake their heads and answer, "No." Then would follow comments like, "That goose would make a tasty morsel." Leopoldina would reply with a series of honkings to ease her terrified heart.

About Elbert, though, they would say, "That's no ordinary dog. There's something special about him." Then they would stroke their beards or fold their arms across their chests or place their fingers reflectively on the side of their noses or cock their heads to the side and silently study him. Finally, they would conclude, "Can't put my finger on it, but there's something different about that dog."

His tags, too, were the subject of much musing and debate. Why would anyone put a leather band with bars of metal on it around a dog's neck? That was the question most of the visitors asked.

"Why, for adornment, of course." responded Aunt Carrie one day, peering at Elbert over the top of her glasses. "Just like Betsy adorned Silly Goose with a blue bow around her neck."

It was a warm July Sunday, and all the family had gathered at the Nichols' for a picnic. Even Aunt Carrie, Uncle Bertram, and their ten-year-old son Harry had come from Downsville the day before so they could enjoy the get-together. Now, after an abundant feast of the best cooking and baking of all the women, they had moved to the shade of the front porch.

"But why all these strange letters and numbers," wondered Cousin Harry, scrutinizing each of the tags. He spelled out the top line of one tag: "NYS AGR and then a strange sign— looks like the sign for *and*, and then MKTS. Then the next line says, 'Albany,

NY.' The NY must mean New York. Do you think maybe he's from Albany?"

"Perhaps somebody from Albany was visiting in the area and brought him along and then he got away from them." Nathaniel's father offered. "We could put a notice in the newspaper."

"And look at the numbers," Betsy said, pushing her head in front of Cousin Harry to read them; "2578372. I bet they're a secret code, and every number stands for a letter, and if we could find the secret code we could read the message.

"Betsy." her mother said sternly. "Your imagination is getting away from you again."

Betsy paid no attention to her mother but went on, "And the next one, that looks like a bell, it says '1990.'" She looked up at the family. "Maybe he's a dog from the future."

"The future!" everyone echoed. Aunt Carrie shook her head and waved her hand hopelessly, as if to say that Betsy was a lost cause.

Nathaniel, who sat on the edge of the porch and kept himself out of the discussion of the tags, spoke up. "You're so dumb, Betsy. It's supposed to be 1890. They just made a mistake."

"How do you know, smartie?" she shot back. "If they made a mistake, seems like they would have fixed it. And look at the next lines," she went on, sounding out the words, " ' Norden Rabies Vac 415002.' Now since you're so smart, tell me what that means."

"I don't know and I don't care," Nathaniel snapped back.

Ignoring his comment, Betsy continued, "I bet pirates captured him in China and brought him to New York City, and if we could figure out the code, we would know who they were and where they buried their treasure. "

"Betsy," her mother interposed, "what have I told you about making up those wild stories?"

"But it could be, Mama," she fought back. "Nobody really knows."

"You spend too much time daydreaming and letting your imagination run wild. You would be better off if you devoted more time to your lessons and your sewing."

Humiliated at being scolded in front of company and hurt by the rejection of her suggestion, Betsy began to cry.

"Enough of this," her father said. "Let the dog alone."

Betsy got up from the grass, where she had been sitting with Elbert and Cousin Harry, and ran into the house.

During this time, Elbert had looked from Betsy to Cousin Harry to the group sitting on the front porch. He wondered why they looked so confused, and he hesitantly wagged his tail from time to time as if to say, "It's all right. There's nothing to worry about."

"Come here, Rover," Nathaniel called softly.

Elbert hurried to his friend, and Nathaniel put his arm around the dog and patted him. "You're my pal," he whispered, and Elbert responded by licking Nathaniel's face.

Nathaniel fingered Elbert's tags. The discussion about them upset him because he was afraid that someone some day would figure out what they meant, and he might have to give up his new friend. He rubbed his thumb slowly over each of the tags. Maybe he ought to take them off the way he had filed off the third tag—the one that said, "Elbert, Finch Hollow Road, Walton, NY." He knew that Finch Hollow Road was up the river just a few miles, and he knew that his father would immediately seek out Mr. Finch and ask if anyone there was missing a dog.

Nathaniel patted Elbert's back. Elbert looked up into his friend's face. He could not see why the tags seemed to matter so much to Nathaniel and Betsy, or why they brought such a sad and worried look into Nathaniel's face. He wagged his tail happily as if to say, "Don't feel so bad. I'm your friend, and that's all that really matters."

With Elbert nestled comfortably across his knees, Nathaniel leaned back against the porch post. The conversation of the family drifted into his consciousness. They were still discussing Elbert.

" . . . couldn't have just come out of nowhere. He must belong to someone," Aunt Carrie was saying.

"You never know how far he's wandered," Uncle Bertram said. "He could be quite far from home, and he can't tell us where home is."

"Wish I had a dog like that," Cousin Harry put in.

"You don't need a dog," Aunt Carrie said. "You have plenty of chores to do without having to take care of a dog, too."

Nathaniel's father leaned his head on the back of his rocking chair and began to rock back and forth slowly. "I remember when I was growing up, we had a dog on the farm. She was just a mongrel, but I loved that dog. We did everything together."

Nathaniel's mother began to rock back and forth with short quick movements. "Like as not," she said, "some lonely child somewhere is weeping for his lost dog."

Her words fell one by one like stones into Nathaniel's heart. He turned them over and over and listened to them again: "Like as not, some lonely child somewhere is weeping for his lost dog."

Nathaniel had never thought about it that way. He had never realized that some boy might be feeling the way he would feel if he lost Rover. He pictured a boy very much like himself, wandering through woods and fields and up and down roads, calling for his dog. He thought of the third tag, hidden on a beam in the barn.

The more the image of the lonely boy searching for his dog remained in Nathaniel's thoughts, the more uneasy he felt. He had to admit the dog did not rightfully belong to him. Perhaps he should tell his father about the third tag so they could go to Finch Hollow Road and search for Elbert's owner. But troubled though he was, Nathaniel said nothing to anyone that day. And Elbert, seeing his friend troubled, grew sad, for he did not know how to comfort him.

Chapter 6

Mr. Fyffe

An answer came to Nathaniel in the person of Mr. Fyffe, who rumbled up the lane in his wagon the next afternoon.

Mr. Fyffe was a tall thin man who walked with long easy strides and whistled his way through life. Sometimes he whistled a rollicking dancing song, but most of the time, his tunes were slow and thoughtful, or sad and wistful and dreamy. Nathaniel's mother said that he whistled all the time because he was lonely. Many years ago, his young wife had died when their first child – a son – was born, and the baby had died, too.

With an old felt hat pulled tightly over his thinning gray hair and its brim shading his bright blue eyes, he strode out to the field where Nathaniel's father and his sons and several other farmers, who had come to help, were following the hay rake that was gathering the freshly cut hay into piles. Then they tossed the hay into the wagon with pitchforks.

As his friend approached, Nathaniel's father paused and wiped his wet face on his sleeve. "Why, Jim," he called, "come join the crowd."

Mr. Fyffe waved his hand. "Sure thing, Alex, "he answered, taking a pitchfork from the wagon and setting to work.

The sight of Mr. Fyffe heartened the downcast Nathaniel, who was working along with the men. He felt sure Mr. Fyffe would be able to help him solve his dilemma.

Mr. Fyffe was not only Nathaniel's father's good friend; he was Nathaniel's, too. Ever since Nathaniel had been old enough to go into the woods, he had spent many happy hours with Mr. Fyffe, learning the ways of nature. Mr. Fyffe taught him how to set traps for lynx and otter, where to find the best fishing holes, and how to bag the sharp-eyed wild turkey.

As the men laid down their pitchforks and set off across the fields for dinner, Nathaniel fell into step with Mr. Fyffe. This was not easy to do, considering the older man's long stride, but Nathaniel kept up as best he could with Elbert romping alongside them.

After a moment, Mr. Fyffe noticed his young friend. "Why, Nathaniel, how is it with you?" he asked, looking down at the boy.

"First rate, Mr. Fyffe," he replied in his best adult-sounding voice. He did not know exactly what "first rate" meant, but it was one of Mr. Fyffe's favorite expressions.

"You're getting to be a regular helper on the farm," Mr. Fyffe said. "Before we know it, you'll be ready to take over."

"Oh, no, Mr. Fyffe. I expect Reuben will take over, but maybe I'll have my own farm some day."

"I do hope so, Nat," Mr. Fyffe replied. "There's nothing like having your own place, even if it is a lot of work."

"Mr. Fyffe, may I ask you a question?"

"Sure thing, Nat. What is it?"

Nathaniel hesitated, then blurted out, "Do you know of anyone by the name of Elbert on Finch Hollow Road?"

Mr. Fyffe stroked his chin thoughtfully for a moment. Then he said, "Can't say as I do, Nat."

"Do you know if anyone is missing a dog there?" Nathaniel asked, rushing the words so that they tumbled over each other as they came out.

"You're still trying to find Rover's owner?" Mr. Fyffe asked.

"Well . . . " Nathaniel hesitated. "If I tell you something, Mr. Fyffe, will you promise not to tell Father?"

"Oh, so it's like that." Mr. Fyffe replied. "Out with it, Nat. What are you up to now?"

"You remember the two metal pieces Rover has on that collar on his neck?"

"That I do," Mr. Fyffe said.

"Well, there really were three."

Mr. Fyffe stopped abruptly. "There were?" What happened to the third one?"

"I filed it off," Nathaniel answered in a subdued voice.

"Now, why did you do that, Nat?" Mr. Fyffe asked, resuming his walk across the field.

"Because of what it said. It said, 'Elbert, Finch Hollow Road, Walton, NY.' "

Mr. Fyffe stroked his chin thoughtfully again. "So you think Rover belongs to someone in Finch Hollow?"

Nathaniel shrugged his shoulders, "I don't know." He was silent for a moment. "Could you help me find out?"

"But why the secrecy? Why don't you tell your father, especially since he'll find out anyway if you have to give the dog back, won't he?"

"If I tell Father, he will say I was trying to steal someone's dog, and he'll be sure mad at me. But if you find the owner, he'll just think you asked around."

"And if we don't find any owner, he need never know about that third tag?"

Nathaniel nodded.

"Well, Nat," Mr. Fyffe went on, "I have an even better idea. Why don't you and Rover come home with me tomorrow morning. We can say we're going to look for Rover's owner in my neck of the woods."

Nathaniel beamed. "Gee, Mr. Fyffe, that's the best idea ever." he cried. "I'm going to ask Mother and Father right now." Then he dashed off toward the house with Elbert close at his heels.

Chapter 7

Finch Hollow

They set off the next morning after breakfast—Mr. Fyffe, Nathaniel, and Elbert. They stopped briefly at Mr. Fyffe's place up the river to water the horse and check with his brother, who helped him on the farm. Then they headed directly for Finch Hollow.

"I owe the Finches a visit," he said to Nathaniel as they rode along the dusty road, "and now is as good a time as any to do it."

They turned from the main road onto Finch Hollow Road under a low gray sky that threatened rain. Fields of corn and oats spread out on either side, along with meadows dotted with grazing cows. The only buildings along the way were two farmhouses with barns and other outbuildings nearby. In the farther fields, several men were cutting hay, trying to finish before the rain came.

As the road began to ascend slowly and the gentle hills on either side to close in just a little more, Elbert, who was sitting on the wagon seat between Mr. Fyffe and Nathaniel, began to feel uneasy. Across his nose passed waves of wet cool air smelling of damp hay and bruised ripened apples and raspberry pie baking in the oven. The odors tingling in his nose confused Elbert. Something strange was in the air—something he was drawn to and yet wanted to run away from. He began to whine and bark. Then he made a leap for the ground, but Nathaniel caught him and held him back.

"What's wrong with you, Rover?" he asked. Then he said to Mr. Fyffe, "Maybe he does live here. Maybe he recognizes the place."

Mr. Fyffe looked at Elbert, who was poised to leap again, but he said nothing.

At last they reached the Finches' home: a large white farmhouse, freshly painted, with green shutters and a wide front porch. It was set back from the road with a row of fir trees on the north side protecting it from the cold winter winds. To the left stood a large barn and several smaller buildings still gleaming from a fresh coat of earthtone red paint. Beyond the house, the apple trees in the orchard hung thick with green fruit. Beyond the orchard, spreading out on all sides toward the mountain, lay the meadows and fields and, at the base of the mountain, a woodlot.

Elbert knew the house. He recognized it as the Tappers' with its old familiar friendly tune seeping up from the musty cellar, slipping through cracks in windows and doors, and swirling around the house. Only now, the melody was in the wrong key.

They turned in at the dusty rutted drive that led to the house. As they stopped by the front porch, a frail middle-aged woman with a thin, pale face and bright brown eyes came out of the house with a broom in her hand. She wore a long gray dress with a high collar and a white apron stained with strawberry juice. Her thin graying hair was gathered in a bun on top of her head.

"Why, hello, Mrs. Finch," Mr. Fyffe said, doffing his hat and climbing down from the wagon.

Nathaniel let go of Elbert, and they both jumped down from the wagon. Leaving Mr. Fyffe to visit with Mrs. Finch, Nathaniel followed Elbert to find out what was upsetting him.

The waves of cool moist air came thicker and faster over Elbert, filled with the scent of pine needles and smooth shiny stones and freshly caught fish. They came over him now like a strong current, threatening to sweep him away. But Elbert fought against them with muscles straining, his four feet planted firmly on the ground. He faced the house as he would an opponent, barking and howling and scolding it for being wrong.

Nathaniel knelt down on the ground beside him and tried to comfort him, but not even his friend's soothing words and warm touch could ease Elbert's disquiet or dispel the strange power pressing in on him.

Suddenly Elbert darted toward the house and raced madly around it several times. Then he began to sniff at doors and cellar windows, and to scratch and dig around a clump of golden glow growing tall near the back door, its yellow blossoms ready to burst open. He searched around the front porch steps for the rhododendron bushes where he had so often snuggled, but the spots were bare. For a few moments, he dug around a lilac bush on the side of the house and scratched his nose on a rosebush climbing up a trellis near the front porch. No matter what he did, he could not find the key to making the place right.

"Nat, bring the dog here," Mr. Fyffe called.

"Come on Rover," Nathaniel said in his most cajoling tone. "Let's see what Mr. Fyffe wants."

Urged on by Nathaniel, Elbert reluctantly came and stood before Mr. Fyffe and Mrs. Finch.

"This is Alex Nichol's son Nathaniel." Mr. Fyffe said to Mrs. Finch. "He found the dog and wants to know if you or anyone in the Hollow lost it."

Mrs. Finch studied Elbert for a moment. "He isn't ours. That I'm sure of," she said. Then she stooped down and stroked Elbert's head and back. He wagged his tail cautiously, hesitantly. He wasn't sure what to make of this woman. She did not have the right scent either. "He's a fine-looking dog," she went on. "Some of the neighbor boys are helping with the haying. Maybe they will know where he came from."

As she stood up, she looked toward the fields. "The men are coming in now. And not a moment too soon," she added as several drops of rain fell upon them. "Won't you and Nat stay to dinner?"

"We sure would be glad to. Thank you, Mrs. Finch," Mr. Fyffe replied, bowing slightly.

At that moment, a long-haired russet-colored dog came racing toward them. "Here's

Rusty," Mrs. Finch laughed. "Come on, Rusty," she called. "Meet our visitors."

But when Rusty caught sight of Elbert, he stopped abruptly and began to growl. In response, Elbert backed closer to Nathaniel and growled. Then Rusty began to bark his warning: "Keep out! This is my territory."

"Come now, Rusty, that's no way to act toward company," Mrs. Finch said.

But Elbert had no more desire to be friends with Rusty than Rusty had to be friends with him. He turned tail and ran to the wagon. Then he looked back at Nathaniel and Mr. Fyffe as if to say, "Let's get out of here."

But Nathaniel and Mr. Fyffe were in no way ready to leave, not with the promise of Mrs. Finch's cooking and the smell of strawberry pie in the kitchen.

With much coaxing, Elbert reluctantly followed Nathaniel toward the house, but at the door, he stopped. When he turned around and saw Rusty close behind, he decided it would be safer to stick close to Nathaniel. So he hurried into the house at his friend's heels.

Mrs. Finch gave Elbert a bowl of food in a corner of the kitchen while Rusty had his outside. The smell and the taste of the food calmed Elbert somewhat, and when he had finished eating, he crept to Nathaniel's place at the table and lay down close beside the boy's feet.

Lying there on the floor, feeling safe and satisfied, Elbert listened to the scraping of chairs on the floor, the clang of pots, the tinkle of dishes, and the talking and laughing of the people above him. And round about and through all the noise, there came from the floor and the walls the song of the house that he had heard outside. Sometimes it swelled to a great crescendo, sometimes it faded away to a faint sigh. But this time, it sounded right. Suddenly a surge of loneliness and homesickness for he knew not what swept over him, and he began to whimper.

Chapter 8

Goose-napped!

Several hours later, Mr. Fyffe set out for home with Nathaniel and Elbert. Mr. Finch, along with the neighboring men and boys, had declared that they had never seen Rover in their territory. "He's not from this neck of the woods," Mr. Finch said, summing up the discussion. Now, with a clear conscience, Nathaniel could claim Elbert as his dog.

As they rode up the lane toward Nathaniel's home, Elbert caught sight of

Leopoldina preening herself by the pond. He leaped from the wagon and raced across the lawn toward her, barking the good news of his return.

Leopoldina, however, did not seem the least bit interested in Elbert and contented herself with strutting up and down to show off the bright blue ribbon tied around her neck.

Disappointed with this poor welcome, Elbert turned away, tail drooping. Leopoldina hurried after him, honking excitedly to tell him she had missed him and was glad he had come back. Then they romped around the pond for some time like the good buddies they were.

This happy life filled several weeks. Then, one quiet sunny afternoon, the shadow of Reuben, Nathaniel's oldest brother, crept across the grass to the pond where Leopoldina was enjoying a siesta. He came upon her so suddenly that he had tucked her under his arm and was walking with long easy strides to the wagon at the edge of the lawn before she realized what was happening.

Quickly Reuben deposited her in the crate in which she had made her first frightening ride to town. She honked and honked, straining against the crate as if she could break it just by pushing. But the crate was solid, and her honking was lost in the rumbling of the wagon as Reuben set off down the road.

Leopoldina knew where she was being taken. She knew the farm road and the turn onto the main road, which Reuben took with such speed that the crate slid across the wagon floor to the farther end. She knew the bridge and the turn up the road past the fields and meadows. She knew the village street with its houses and shops and offices. She knew Reuben was taking her to the Widow Blair.

When Reuben pulled up in front of the Widow Blair's gate, Leopoldina grew even more frantic and strained once more against her prison.

The Widow was sweeping the front porch, but she paused and leaned on her broom as Reuben approached with the crate and its honking occupant.

"Good afternoon, Mrs. Blair," he called as he came up the sidewalk.

"Good afternoon, Reuben. Is that the goose your father brought to me some weeks ago?"

"Yes, it is."

She propped her broom against a rocking chair and came closer. "So you found no owner for her?"

"No, we didn't. Would you like to buy her? Father said you could use her."

"I could, Reuben. She would make a nice roast for my guests who are coming next week. And I do need some more feathers to finish stuffing the pillows for Amanda Jennings' wedding present." She hesitated. "But didn't your father promise her to Betsy?"

Reuben shrugged his shoulders. "He didn't tell me that," he answered.

"Perhaps Betsy lost interest in the goose," the Widow said. She tucked into her white cap some stray hairs that floated around her face. Then she rolled up her sleeves as if she were preparing to do the dishes. "Now what are you asking for her?"

Reuben shrugged his shoulders again. "Fifty cents?"

The Widow shook her head slowly, her face drooping. "Oh my, Reuben, a poor widow like me could never afford that."

Reuben bit his lip and set the crate on the ground. "Would 30¢ do?" he asked.

"I couldn't go above 25¢," she answered. "Come in and I will see if I have that much."

She led the way through the best parlor and the darkened dining room and into the kitchen. Then she disappeared behind the dark flowered drapes that covered the entrance to the pantry. She pushed her way through several rows of home-canned applesauce and cherries, until she reached an old chipped sugar bowl. Digging through the coins lightly jingling inside, she took out two dimes and a nickel. As she came back into the kitchen, she said, "There you are," and handed the coins to Reuben.

He pocketed them and grinned. "Thank you, Mrs. Blair, thank you. Would you like me to take the goose out to the meadow for you?"

"That I would, Reuben," she answered. "And did your father tell you about fixing my roof?"

"Oh, yes, he said I was to fix it for you today."

The Widow clasped her hands together under her chin. "Oh, you and your father are such a blessing for a poor widow woman like me," she said. "But come, let's have the goose out in the meadow with the others."

Chapter 9

A New Meadow

As soon as Reuben lifted the lid of the crate, Leopoldina bolted out. She stood dazed and frightened in the wide expanse of meadow, not knowing what to do.

The other geese were a short distance away near the brook, but a few saw her and came toward her, honking. Two of them came alongside of her and began to walk straight ahead. Then they stopped and turned around to look at her, meaning that she should follow them.

Hesitantly, Leopoldina followed her escorts. They led her to the brook and dipped their bills into the refreshing water. She followed their lead. The cool water flowing down her throat felt good. It calmed her fears and set her frightened heart free.

She lifted her head from the water and looked around at the friends that surrounded her. Then she looked around at the meadow stretching out on all sides. She felt the soothing sweep of a gentle breeze across her feathers. Suddenly, it felt good to be alive. With a free heart, she began to strut across the meadow with her new companions, not realizing that she was the only goose wearing a wide blue ribbon tied in a bow around her neck.

Chapter 10

Missing Leopoldina

It had not been a good afternoon for Elbert.

With tail dragging, he had followed Nathaniel through the woods. "Go, get 'em, boy!" Nathaniel urged again and again. But all this encouragement failed to stir up Elbert's usual excitement for a fleeing rabbit.

Frustrated by his listless hunting companion, Nathaniel sat down on a rock and took Elbert's face in his hands. "What's wrong with you today, Rover?" he asked, studying the dog's mournful eyes.

In response, Elbert whimpered, then settled down at Nathaniel's feet with his head on his paws.

"We better go home," Nathaniel finally said, rising and setting off down the hill.

When they reached the farm, Elbert hurried to the pond to find Leopoldina. He wandered all along the edge, sniffing the grass and weeds. He picked up her scent strongly, but he caught Reuben's, too. He traced both of them to the road where the wagon had stood. Then he lost them.

Frantic, he began to race from place to place around the house and barn, sniffing, searching. When he could find no scent of them, he knew that Leopoldina had been taken away by Reuben.

Immediately, he dashed down the farm road, turned into the main road, and sped as fast as his legs would carry him into the village and the Widow Blair's.

Chapter 11

A Confession

When Nathaniel took his supper out to him that evening, Elbert did not come running. In fact, he was nowhere in sight.

"Here, Rover!" Nathaniel called. Then he whistled and called again. "Where could that dog be?" he muttered as he walked around the house and barn, calling and whistling. When he went down to the pond, he discovered that Leopoldina was missing, too.

"Nat, come get your supper or it'll all be cold," his mother called from the back porch.

Nathaniel came into the kitchen and said, "I can't find Rover, and Betsy's goose is gone, too."

Betsy and her older sister Jennie were visiting their grandmother on another farm and would not return until the next morning. The rest of the family responded with surprise and many questions and comments.

David, one of Nathaniel's older brothers, said, "Perhaps whoever they belong to came by and saw them and took them back."

"Something is wrong I know," Nathaniel said, "because Rover just wasn't himself today."

Reuben said nothing but ate steadily, his eyes fixed on his plate.

Finally, his mother said to him, "Reuben, have you seen the goose or the dog?"

Reuben glanced briefly at his mother, then lowered his eyes again.

"I did not see either of them when I came in to supper," he said.

The next morning, when Betsy and Jennie came rumbling up the road, Nathaniel went out to meet them. Betsy jumped from the wagon and ran across the lawn, bubbling over with news of her visit.

"Look at the beautiful doll Grandmother gave me," she shouted, holding out a doll with a painted china face and eyes that opened and closed. "And Jennie got a beautiful old quilt that Grandmother's friends made for her when she was married. "

Nathaniel could not find a wedge for his message about the goose, so he followed Betsy as she ran into the house to pour out her joy to her mother.

"Finally, she said, "I'm going out to see Silly Goose. I bet she missed me."

Nathaniel and his mother looked at each other for a moment.

Then his mother said, "I'm afraid Silly Goose has disappeared. "

"Disappeared?" Betsy repeated. "How could she disappear? "

"I don't know, dear," her mother answered. "But we missed her yesterday at suppertime, and since daybreak, Nathaniel has been searching the farm and the woods for her and Rover. He has disappeared, too."

Without a word, Betsy dashed from the house and ran down to the pond. "Silly Goose! Silly Goose!" she called over and over. She walked all around the pond and, parting the weeds and cattails, peered into the growth around the water. Finally, she sat down at the edge of the pond and sobbed.

That night at supper, Nathaniel was somber and silent, while Betsy twirled her fork around and around in her mashed potatoes, a faraway look in her eyes.

"Betsy, stop playing with your food and eat," her mother said.

"I'm not hungry."

"Whether you're hungry or not, you have to eat something," her mother insisted.

Betsy gathered some potatoes on the edge of her fork and put it into her mouth.

"Mama," she began after she had swallowed the potatoes, "do you think the Widow Blair came and stole Silly Goose?"

Her mother turned to her from little Rachel, who was in her highchair, throwing peas from her plate onto the floor. "Of course not, Betsy. She wouldn't do a thing like that."

Her father, Reuben, and David had been discussing a problem they were having with one of the cows, but her father suddenly stopped and looked toward Betsy. "Betsy," he said, "the Widow Blair knew I had promised the goose to you. I will not have you imputing evil deeds to her or to anyone. Now let's hear no more about this."

Betsy said no more, but the thought of Silly Goose occupied her mind well into the night. The next morning, when she came down for breakfast, her father had not yet come in from milking the cows.

She came and stood next to her mother, who was at the stove, turning pancakes over in a large black skillet.

"Mama," she began in a low hesitant voice, "may I say something about Silly Goose?"

Her mother studied Betsy's face a moment, then turned to the pancakes. "Yes, dear. What is it?"

"Maybe Silly Goose wandered away and someone took her to the Widow Blair just like Papa did when she first came."

"That could very well have happened," her mother answered.

"Could we go and ask her?"

"I suppose we could do that," her mother said, "but I don't know when we will next get to the village."

At that moment, her father walked in. "What's this about going to the village?" he asked, sitting down at the table.

Reuben, David, and Nathaniel came in and sat down in their places.

Her mother took a large platter from the cupboard and returned to the skillet of pancakes. "Betsy would like to go and ask the Widow Blair if anyone brought in Silly Goose."

Her father frowned at Betsy. "Did you forget what I told you last night?"

"No, Papa," she murmured. "But I'm not blaming the Widow. I thought maybe somebody found Silly Goose and took her to the Widow Blair, just like you did."

Her father was silent for a moment. "That sounds reasonable. There would be no harm in asking her. In fact, when I go into the village tomorrow, I'll ask around."

"And Rover, too," Nathaniel added.

"They came together so they may be lost together," his father added.

Reuben had sat silently during this conversation, his eyes on the tablecloth. Suddenly he looked up and said, "I sold the goose to the Widow Blair."

For a moment, everyone was caught in stunned silence. His mother stood over the stove, ready to lift pancakes from the skillet into the platter. "Reuben, you didn't!" she half whispered, setting the pancake turner and the empty platter on the table.

Nathaniel was too shocked to speak, but Betsy, in tears, blurted out, "She was mine. You had no right to take her away and sell her."

His father, face white, said with deliberate calm, "And with what authority did you do this?"

Reuben squirmed in his chair. "No one had claimed her, and she only hung around the house and made noise and made the yard dirty."

"How much did the Widow pay you?" his father continued in the same deadly tone.

"Twenty-five cents."

"And what did you do with the 25¢?"

"I put it toward the price of my colt," he answered. All this time, he had kept his head down. Now he looked up at his father. "I needed only 50¢ more to pay for the colt."

His father banged his fist on the table so that the knives, forks, and spoons jumped in their places, and the cups rattled in their saucers. "And so . . . a colt was more valuable to you than just and honest dealings with your neighbors?"

"But I was not dishonest with the Widow," Reuben protested.

"The goose was not yours to sell." his father reminded him. "Did I not teach you to deal honestly and fairly? Has everything I taught you gone for naught? I thought you were a man. I praised you through the whole countryside as a man who could take over and handle the business of the farm. But you are no man or a son of mine. You are a scoundrel . . . a disgrace!"

He paused to catch his breath. Only the ticking of the clock on the wall behind him could be heard, cutting through the heavy silence. Then he went on. "There will be no colt. You may go to Mr. Fyffe today and tell him he is free to sell it to someone else."

Reuben faced his father again. "But, Father, I worked hard to earn the money for it, and I need only 25¢ more."

"There will be no colt," his father repeated evenly, emphatically. "If that colt means so much to you that you would stoop to selling what you had no right to sell, then it is not worth having. There will be no colt."

While his father was scolding Reuben, Nathaniel's mind was working. He remembered what the Widow had said when he and his father had first gone to her with Leopoldina.

"Father," he said, "the Widow said she would like the goose to make a roast for her guests, who were coming soon, and she needed feathers to finish Amanda Jennings' pillows for her wedding. We ought to go quickly to save her."

Betsy sprang from her chair. "Let's hurry and rescue her before it's too late," she cried.

She and Nathaniel started for the door. "Just a minute, children," their father said, holding up his hand. "How are you going to get there?"

Nathaniel shrugged. "We can run. We've got to hurry before it's too late."

"Sit down and eat your breakfast. Then Reuben will take you promptly to the village. He needs to apologize to the Widow and give back her 25¢."

Reuben looked up and opened his mouth to speak, but sensing that protest was useless, closed it again and settled down to contemplating his plate until the pancakes were served.

After breakfast, Reuben, sullen and silent, hitched Nellie to the wagon and set off with Nathaniel and Betsy for the Widow Blair's.

Chapter 12

Foiled Rescue

When Elbert reached the Widow Blair's, the afternoon shadows were lengthening, and the day had a worn look. Urged on by her call, the Widow's flock of geese were already marching toward her backyard. Soon they would make their way to their coop and settle down for the night.

Elbert nosed around the Widow's front fence and gate. He paused before an opening made by a missing board, then decided against trying to squeeze through it. Instead, he followed the fence around the Widow's property to the back. The noise of the returning geese shattered the quiet of the early evening. As he turned the corner at the back, Elbert immediately spotted Leopoldina, strutting proudly with her bright blue bow, completely at home with her new friends.

When she saw Elbert, Leopoldina hurried toward him, honking about her new-found joy. He, in turn, began to wag his tail and bounded toward her. But he stopped short as five or six of the flock turned and followed Leopoldina. Elbert backed off, tail drooping, and barked from what seemed a safe distance.

The Widow, disturbed by this complication to her evening ritual of gathering in the geese, came after them with a long rough stick. She prodded the wandering geese to go toward the back gate. Then she waved the stick at Elbert. "Scat! " she hissed. "Go away!"

Elbert retreated a little farther, still unwilling to lose sight of Leopoldina. But she turned with the others and hurried in front of the Widow into the yard. Then the Widow closed and locked the gate.

Elbert was distressed. He had come all this distance to rescue Leopoldina, and the opportunity had slipped by in a flash. But tomorrow would come, and he would wait for it. He lay down outside the Widow's back gate, and there, morning found him, wet with dew and shivering in the chilly morning air.

Chapter 13

Under the Hatchet

Elbert awoke with a gnawing in his stomach. He got up stiffly, shivering and dazed by the strange surroundings. The dew-soaked meadow glinting in the morning sun and the brook murmuring through it in the distance gave the world an unreal, almost eerie, feeling.

Since he had missed supper the night before, Elbert was hungry. He sniffed along the edge of the fence without finding anything to eat. Just then, however, life began to stir inside the Widow's yard. Elbert could hear her moving across the grass and talking to the geese. Their honking cleared his mind, and he remembered why he was there.

The back gate opened at last, and the geese came running out. Elbert watched them go, but his friend with her blue bow was not among them. He walked toward the gate to look for her inside the yard. But the Widow pushed the gate shut so quickly, she almost caught the edge of his nose. "Scat! " she said, waving her hand at him. "Go away! "

But how could he go away when his friend was locked inside? And how could he go away when he was hungry? Even after the Widow turned and disappeared from sight, he stood looking at the gate as if by magic it would suddenly open again.

Finally, with tail drooping, he turned and walked along the fence, sniffing and searching for an opening. As he neared the end of the fence, he caught a tantalizing odor coming from the next yard. It grew stronger and stronger as he came closer. No fence enclosed this yard, and near the back steps was sitting a huge pot from which the odor came.

Delighted with his good fortune, Elbert hurried to the pot and plunged his nose into it, gulping as fast as he could.

"Hey, you! That's for Mr. Sprague's pigs."

Elbert looked up at a young woman who had come out the back door of the house with a large pan. She came down the steps and poured the contents of the pan into the pot.

Elbert dived in again. The woman watched him for a moment. "You sure are hungry," she said. "And I expect you'll be wanting some water, too."

She went back into the house and returned with a pan of water, which she set down next to the pot. When Elbert finally took his snout from the pot and licked his chops clean, he attacked the water with the same gusto, lapping it up with long loud slurps.

Now he was ready to continue his search for Leopoldina. He returned to the fence. The back gate was still closed, but he could hear honking inside. So he began again to search for some way into the Widow's yard. He tried to squeeze between several loose boards in the side fence, but he could not fit between them. Finally, he ran to the front.

There he found a space where two boards were missing, but again, the space was too small. Farther along, near the gate, he found a wider space, and a loose board next to it widened it a little more.

Elbert thrust his head in and pushed against the boards, but he still could not go through the space. As he stood there struggling, he caught sight of Leopoldina's blue bow. The Widow had his friend in her arms. Then she bent over and placed Leopoldina's neck on a block of wood. In her right hand, the blade of a large hatchet flashed.

Elbert pushed frantically at the space, but only wedged himself in more tightly. Just then, a wagon came rumbling down the road and stopped in front of the Widow's gate. "Stop! Stop! Don't hurt Silly Goose!" Nathaniel and Betsy screamed. They tumbled from the wagon and rushed through the gate. Elbert wrenched himself free, and pain shot through him as the wood scraped and tore his shoulders. Then he dashed through the gate with the two children.

The Widow, stooping over Leopoldina, raised the hatchet above the captive goose's head. "Stop! Stop!" the children cried as they ran across the lawn.

Startled, the Widow lowered the hatchet, but with her other hand, she still held firmly onto Leopoldina. Elbert dashed ahead of the running children, grabbed the Widow's skirt between his teeth, and pulled with all his strength.

As the threads holding her skirt together broke, the Widow cried out, lost her balance, and fell, dropping the hatchet and letting go of Leopoldina.

"How did that nasty dog get in here?" she cried.

As soon as the Widow's hold on her was loosed, Leopoldina shot out across the lawn, half-running, half-flying toward the front gate. She had one frantic thought in mind: escape from the Widow Blair.

Betsy ran after her, calling, "Come here, Silly Goose!" But Leopoldina wasn't listening to anyone. She dashed out the gate and into the path of an approaching wagon. The driver pulled his horse up short, just as Betsy caught up with Leopoldina and snatched her from collision with the front wagon wheel.

"What a scare you gave us," she said to Leopoldina as she stroked the frightened goose.

With Reuben's help, Betsy put Leopoldina into the crate for the ride home. Nathaniel led Elbert away from the Widow Blair, at whom he was still snarling and growling, while Reuben settled with the Widow. Then they all set off for the quiet and peace of the farm.

Chapter 14

Heading Home

To all appearances, life on the Nichol farm had returned to normal. Elbert still faithfully followed at Nathaniel's heels wherever he went. Leopoldina basked in the sun at the pond and submitted cheerfully to all of Betsy's wild ideas.

But something had changed since Leopoldina's close encounter with the roasting pan. Even when the sky seemed to be a friendly blue ocean with a toasty July sun sailing over it, a chill wind blew from the North for Elbert and Leopoldina, and the air was filled with the scent of dark storm clouds gathering. The two friends moved restlessly about the farm and ate uneasily, looking about fearfully every now and then, as if they expected some unknown danger to appear suddenly.

Finally, one morning when he awoke, Elbert knew they had to go. Where, he did not know; but the storm clouds smelled sharp and bitter, and pressed upon him heavily.

The sun was not yet up, but light was beginning to filter through the darkness. He left the corner of the back porch where he slept and hurried across the wet grass to the pond. He nudged Leopoldina to wake her. Dazed, she lifted her head and looked about. Then she felt the storm clouds, too, and knew why Elbert had awakened her.

Together they set off across the freshly mowed meadow. At first, they walked side by side, but the farther they went, the faster they walked, until Elbert finally began to run. Leopoldina struggled to keep up with him, half-running, half-flying.

They headed for the woods that lay on the other side of the meadow. As they ran, the day grew brighter and brighter, and the sun appeared low in the east.

When he reached the woods, Elbert stopped, panting, and waited for Leopoldina to catch up with him. Then they set off through the shadows of the trees at a slower pace. Suddenly, they felt a strangeness in the air running over them like rain. Elbert sniffed and sniffed. Leopoldina looked from side to side and honked lightly. It was a wetness like dew falling. It was a sweet juicy bone lying in the grass. It was butterflies and bumblebees and clover brushing over your feet.

From somewhere in the distance, a boy's voice rang out: "Elbert! Leopoldina!" over and over.

The voice seemed to come from far away, floating like bubbles on the wind. Elbert began to run in the direction from which the bubbles came, and Leopoldina hurried after him.

In a few moments, they emerged into the sunlight at the edge of a field of alfalfa.

At the opposite edge, a boy was standing and calling through his hands cupped around his mouth: "Elbert! Leopoldina!"

Elbert plunged into the alfalfa, and Leopoldina followed him. The boy rushed toward them, and they met in a flurry of barking and honking and laughing and tail wagging.

"Where have you been?" he cried, hugging each of them in turn. "We've searched all over for you. Even the police were helping and the radio station."

Then he paused and looked at Leopoldina. "There's something different about you," he said. He studied her for a moment. "Say, where did you get that blue ribbon around your neck?" he asked.

Leopoldina honked and honked, for that was her only way to say, "Do you know the Widow Blair had my neck in her hands and was about to cut off my head?"

But, of course, this boy knew nothing about the Widow Blair and what it was like to have narrowly escaped being a cooked goose or feathers for a pillow.

Then the boy noticed the scrapes on Elbert's shoulders, which had not yet completely healed. He rubbed his hand gently over them, studying them. "Wherever were you, Elbert," he said at last, "to get cut up so?" As his hand brushed against Elbert's tags, he stopped suddenly and examined them.

"Why, your identification tag is missing!" he said. "Did someone steal you? I bet that's how you got those scrapes." Then he hugged Elbert and added, "I'm glad you escaped."

The boy stood up. "Come on, let's go home. Mom and Dad will be glad to hear you're back. They've searched awful hard for you."

As they all turned and set off through the field, Elbert suddenly stopped and looked back toward the woods as if he had forgotten something. He took a few hesitant steps in that direction. Then he looked back at the boy, who had stopped, too, and was urging him to come. He looked again toward the woods and then back again to the boy in blue jeans and a white tee shirt and dirty sneakers with untied laces and his cap slung backwards on his head.

"Come on, Elbert," the boy said. "I'm your friend, Skip. Don't you remember me? Don't you remember going for rides in the car with me and exploring the woods with me?"

Finally, Elbert followed the boy's coaxing and fell into step with him, a little slowly, a little thoughtfully. Perhaps he was remembering chasing rabbits with another boy in dirty overalls and a ragged-edged straw hat with a strand of grass hanging from the corner of his mouth—a boy who lived far far away in another time where Elbert might not ever go again.

Acknowledgments

This story has my name on it, but it was brought to full bloom with the help of friends, relatives, and colleagues who generously read the manuscript and offered suggestions from a missing comma to glaring omissions to just plain support and encouragement.

I offer my deepest thanks to:

My friend Mary Ann Sturm for consultations, creative ideas, proofreading, and especially for believing in my story and giving me endless infusions of encouragement and support.

My friend the late Ken Sprague for farming details, and for trips to observe geese and to tour the real Finch Hollow.

My sister, Marie Lauzau, for her support of my writing, and to Marie and her husband Ron for helping make this publication possible.

Barbara Dauria of Touchstone Graphics for being such a patient, careful, encouraging, and pleasant person to work with in bringing this book into existence.

My friend the late Stephen Grosso for recommending me to Barbara Dauria and encouraging me in my writing career.

My friend Helen Casey for passing her "eagle eye" over the manuscript and offering suggestions for improvement, and for helping to find my artist.

Annie James who enthusiastically offered to do the illustrations and worked at them with care, dedication, and patience.

Ann Smith for providing the information for Elbert's tags.

My cousins, Jill and Mark Quigley, who read the manuscript and look forward to its publication.

Peira and Keaton Christiansen, who read the manuscript when they were children and offered some excellent suggestions (which I followed).

And to all my young readers:

SPECIAL THANKS !

102

Dorothy Kubik, a retired English teacher, is a free-lance writer who lives in Hamden, New York, with her cat, Jane. Ever since she moved to the Catskills in 1973, she has enjoyed studying and writing about local history.

She has written many articles and two books on hisorical subjects: *A Free Soil – A Free People: the Anti-Rent War in Delaware County, New York* and *West Through the Catskills: The Story of the Susquehanna Turnpike.*

The Adventures of Elbert and Leopoldina is her first book for children.

To purchase books by Dorothy Kubik:

LOOK AT AND PURCHASE BOOKS (save time + shipping charges):

AT: The Telecenter
254 Main Street, Oneonta, NY 13820
(607) 431-6000

OR: The Delaware County Historical Association
46549 State Route 10, Delhi, NY 13753
(607) 746-3849

The Adventures of Elbert and Leopoldina

ORDER FROM:
Echo Farm Publications   607-865-8351
8058 County Highway 26, Hamden, New York 13782

A Free Soil – A Free People:
The Anti-Rent War in Delaware County, New York

ORDER FROM:
Echo Farm Publications   607-865-8351
8058 County Highway 26, Hamden, New York 13782

OR: Purple Mountain Press   1 - 800- 325-2665
PO Box 309, Fleischmanns, NY 12430-0309

West Through the Catskills:
The Story of the Susquehanna Turnpike

ORDER FROM:
Echo Farm Publications   607-865-8351
8058 County Highway 26, Hamden, New York 13782

OR: Purple Mountain Press   1 - 800- 325-2665
PO Box 309, Fleischmanns, NY 12430-0309

CHECK OUT: TouchstoneGraphics.com/bookinfo
to find us on the internet.

To purchase books by Dorothy Kubik:

LOOK AT AND PURCHASE BOOKS (save time + shipping charges):

AT: The Telecenter
254 Main Street, Oneonta, NY 13820
(607) 431-6000

OR: The Delaware County Historical Association
46549 State Route 10, Delhi, NY 13753
(607) 746-3849

The Adventures of Elbert and Leopoldina

ORDER FROM:
Echo Farm Publications   607-865-8351
8058 County Highway 26, Hamden, New York 13782

A Free Soil – A Free People:
The Anti-Rent War in Delaware County, New York
ORDER FROM:
Echo Farm Publications   607-865-8351
8058 County Highway 26, Hamden, New York 13782

OR: Purple Mountain Press   1 - 800- 325-2665
PO Box 309, Fleischmanns, NY 12430-0309

West Through the Catskills:
The Story of the Susquehanna Turnpike
ORDER FROM:
Echo Farm Publications   607-865-8351
8058 County Highway 26, Hamden, New York 13782

OR: Purple Mountain Press   1 - 800- 325-2665
PO Box 309, Fleischmanns, NY 12430-0309

CHECK OUT: TouchstoneGraphics.com/bookinfo
to find us on the internet.